Well Done, Dougal!

Benedict Blathwayt

RED FOX

cat

lighthouse

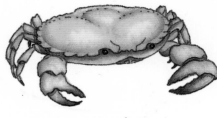

crab

harbour master

fishing boat

Dougal's driver

rope

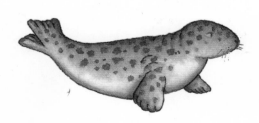

seal

seaweed

seagull

clock tower

Patch

Dougal

warning buoy

foreman

motor boat

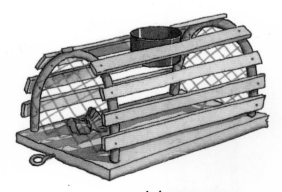

lobster pot

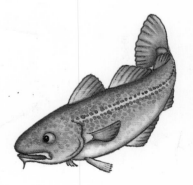

fish

Dougal the Digger was down at the harbour digging a trench for new drains.

The foreman and his dog Patch were there too.

Some children from the village were going
fishing. Patch wanted to go as well.

"Keep clear of the red warning flags,"
the harbour master reminded them.
"It gets very shallow out there at low tide."

In the morning the tide came right in.

In the afternoon the tide
began to go out again.

Suddenly there was a lot of shouting and barking from the middle of the bay. On their way home, the children had run aground.

"That mud is deep and dangerous stuff," said the harbour master, shaking his head. "Unless we get them off soon they'll be stuck until tonight's high tide – and it's going to get very dark and cold out there."

They **threw** a long rope to the boat.

They all tried
to pull the boat off
the mud – but it was hopeless.

They pulled and pulled and pulled

. . . but the boat stayed stuck.

Then the harbour master had an idea.
He tied the rope to the back of Dougal.
"It's up to you now, Dougal," he said.

Dougal's fat tyres gripped the harbour road.
The rope grew tighter and tighter and tighter.

Dougal's engine ROARED ...

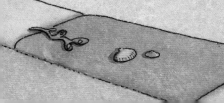

Then SHLOOOP!

The boat suddenly slid off the mud into the water with a great big SPLASH!

"Hooray!" shouted everyone when the children were safely back on dry land.

"All thanks to Dougal!" smiled the harbour master. "Yes," said the children. **"Well done, Dougal!"**

Woof, woof! barked Patch.